D0923385

FAE and the MOON

To Ivette, for her steadfast support in doing what
I love and always helping me reach for the moon

—FA

Dedicated to our parents, Barbara and Eugene,
and our sister and niece, Megan and Ada

—CS & SS

yellowjacketreads.com

ISBN 978-1-4998-1327-2 (pb) 10 9 8 7 6 5 4 3 2 1 | ISBN 978-1-4998-1328-9 (hc) 10 9 8 7 6 5 4 3 2 1 | ISBN 978-1-4998-1329-6 (eb)

New York, NY | Library of Congress Cataloging-in-Publication Data is available upon request.
First Edition | Manufactured in China RRD 0922

For information about special discounts on bulk purchases, please contact Little Bee Books at sales@littlebeebooks.com.

and the MOON

FRANCO
CATHERINE &
SARAH SATRUN

Sigh

I'm sad...

Nothing changes. Each night I'm hopeful it will...

But it doesn't. She's not here and it makes me angry... but really...

...I'm just sad.

Mother would always say the moon reminded her of me. She would always call me her moon.

Mother loved the moon.

She loved the moon so much she planted a moon garden when we first moved here.

I barely remember it in full bloom.

Where is she?

She would never have abandoned me...
...it's so lonely without Mother...

Fae... Fae...
Always remember...
Mother loves you
very much.
I will
always be
with you.
Mother?
Is that
you?
Where
are you?
Mother?
I can't reach
you!
Mother!

Mother!
Where are
you?
HELP!
Mother!
Mom!
I'm here!
MOM!
MOTHER!

Mom!
MOM!

Fae?
Oh... hey Percival.

How are you?

Hmmm? Oh, I'm fine.

No...
You're not. It's obvious.

The dream again? You know it's not real—
It is real! I saw it...
She's not dead.
She can't be...
At least I don't think she is.
Fae... It's hard to let go.
She's been your entire world your whole life.
Think about why your mother brought you here.
Everything she endured...
The... monsters she escaped to bring you to this warm and loving home she built for the two of you.

I know the stories...
Your mother always looked to the moon for guidance.
She would tell me how beautiful it was.
She would tell me about the different phases and the different interpretations and what they meant to her.
And even stranger stories of fantastical beasts, like dragons, that roamed the sky on moonless nights.
How some creatures shied away from the moon...
...and how others fed off its light.
Sounds dark and dreary.

Not all of her stories were.
She would tell me fairy tales about the sun, the rain, and the moon.

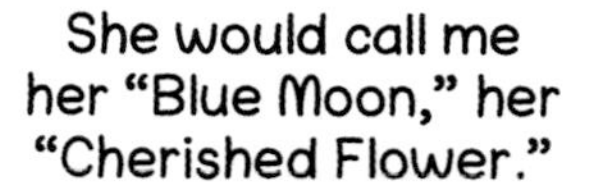
She would call me her “Blue Moon,” her “Cherished Flower.”

She even planted a blue rose in the moon garden and told me it was a symbol of how I was her little miracle.
She told me so many stories...

You think she made up those monster stories?

You think they’re real?

...you are safe now, if that is what worries you.

Safe?

We're not safe.
My mother is missing!

She's not safe! She's out there somewhere, alone.
Maybe she just... left.

Someone took her! I know it!

She has been known to be a bit of a nomad. It's how she got here... with you.

She wouldn't do that to me.
I can feel her... she's still out there somewhere.
Someone... or something has her.

You told me about this before. Are you sure this isn't just your imagination?

Maybe all those stories she told weren't real, but I saw **something**—
I didn't dream it. It wasn't a dream.

I don't know what to believe anymore.

You should believe in her memory. You need to believe in the spirit of her. What she said. What she believed in.
Grab hold of it and don't let go.
Take strength from it by holding it close to your heart...
Do something that will honor her memory.

Eat something. Get some rest.
There's a full moon out tonight and a brand new beginning tomorrow.

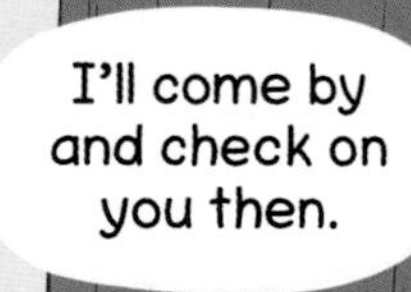
I'll come by and check on you then.

Easy for him to say.

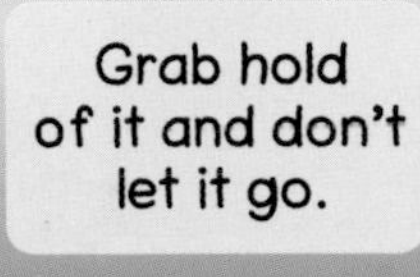
Grab hold of it and don't let it go.

Do something that will honor her memory.

Do something for her...

Let her know I'm still here.

What if I did something she had to see?
Something so big she just has to notice!

If Mother is out there, she has to notice the moon is missing in the sky.

She will come looking for it... for both of us.
She just has to.

CHOP
CHOP
CHOP
Oh! Good morning, Frik. Good morning, Frak.
There you guys are! Where did you off and disappear to last night?
Sorry I've been neglecting you lately.
I think things are looking up for everyone!
MUNCH
MUNCH
MUNCH

Took all day to clean out this garden!

It's been ignored far too long...

Oh. The neighbors? Where are they going?
Are they moving?

They're not the only ones.

Oh, hey Percival.

There will be a lot more leaving in the next few days, I suspect.

Why?
Where are they all going?
Some place safe.
Not that there is any such place, according to some of them.
They're scared.
What? Why?
You didn't notice? Last night? The moon?

Uh, no, what happened to the moon?

It disappeared. Just up and vanished... **poof!**

People are taking it as an evil omen. They say the bad things that have always been kept away because of the light of the moon will now be able to travel under the cover of complete darkness.

It's all superstitious mumbo jumbo to me but people seem very frightened...
You know what I mean, "made-up stories."

Hey. I just realized you're out here in the garden.
You're feeling better. What happened?

What? Oh. Nothing.
I just took your advice. I should be happy. Mom left me so many wonderful memories.

Why are the animals acting weird?

Probably the same thing that has the humans spooked.

Hmmm. It's a pity your mom's moon garden will go to waste without a moon and all...
You should get inside before night hits just in case the moon decides not to show up again. Just to be on the safe side. Would you like me to stay with you?
What? No. I'm sure everything will be fine.

People? Animals? They're all leaving because of the moon?

No Frik and Frak either.
Did you guys move out too?

Hmmmm... House is totally empty.

Mom

Mom's old scrap book.
Mom
Memories

Fae, my sweet,
look what has bloomed
in our moon garden.

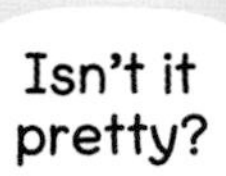

Your first word!

You are my special little flower!
This is a sign, my little cute one!

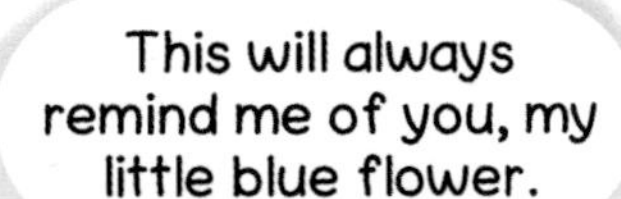
The blue rose is a rare and special thing...
It blooms only with a good healthy dose of moonlight.
We'll place it in this book so we can look upon it through the years.

Rare and special, just like my little girl.

This will always remind me of you, my little blue flower.
Memories

Hey...

There's no sounds out there.

Why is it so quiet—
BANG!

Oh!

There you guys are!
I was starting to get worried you guys packed up and left like the others today.
Why do you guys keep disappearing at night?

But you're here tonight, which is great, because I could really use the company.
I'll just whip us up something to eat and we can spend the rest—

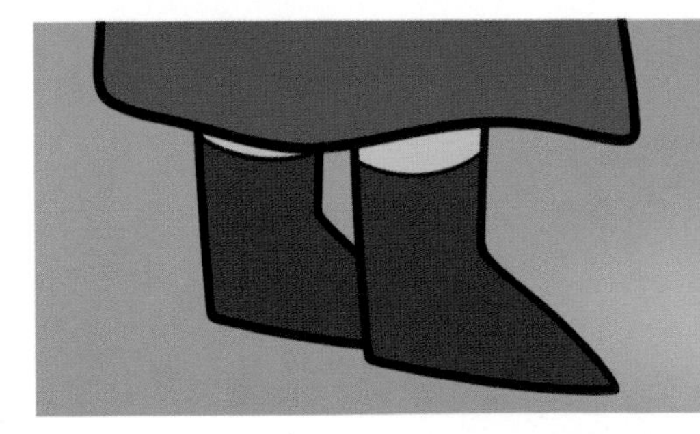
Hey! Where did you go?

That's weird...

THWUMP!
Ah! What the heck was that?
Sounds like a tree fell on the house!

THUMP!
THUMP!
THUMP!
Is... is... someone there?
SHRACCH!

Hello...
I see you there, standing under the midnight...

Where is it?
You... You're real?
Dragons are real!

It was you...

What did you do?

Where is she?

SNARL!
ROAR!
STOP YOUR NONSENSE!

SNIFF
SNIFF

SNIFF
SNIFF

This is I'Lette's home... but you are not her!

I know it's here... I can smell it!
Where are you hiding it?

Hiding? Hiding what?

Stop playing with me, little creature!

THE MOON!
I know it's here!

Your eyes betray you!

Give it to me!
NO!

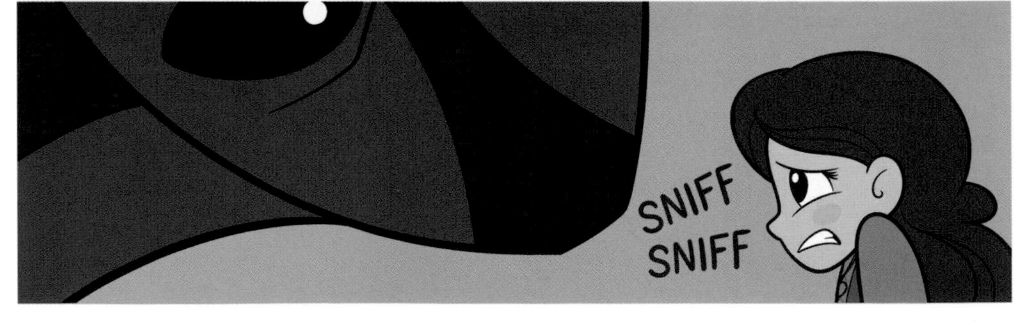
SNIFF SNIFF

No matter where you put it, I will find that moon!

WOOOSH

It’s gone...

What is happening?

How did this get here?
CRACK!
CRACK!
CRACK!
Whoa!
CRACK!
Oooof!
Where... where am I?

It's so dark...
Eyes are finally adjusting.

I'm in a tunnel?
This is directly beneath my house?

Hey. This looks like one of my forks.

And there's my missing hand mirror...
And a spoon...
And my missing sewing kit.

What is this—wait!
It's you two! You took the moon!

What did you do with it?
I want it back right now!

Come back here!

I want the moon back!

I can't see anything...
Hey! Where did you go?
Did it get darker in here?

Frik?
Frak?
Is that you?
Uh...
I think—
I better—

NO!
STAY BACK!
AHH—

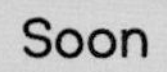
Soon
Where... where am I?

Hey! That's bright!
Why am I tied up?
Who is doing this?

So many questions.

Who am I?

Where is the Moon?

I have some answers...
I am the Rat King!
You stole the Moon!
And *I* want it!

I don't understand—

Enough of this silliness! You are in the dark depths now!

The bowels of the earth!

I... we... are the **vermin** of the earth.
Surface dwellers can't stand to look at us so they chase us with brooms!
We scurry and hide but are always there... just under the surface.

But today that changes!
Because, young lady, YOU stole the Moon right out of the sky!

The Moon means **power** for us... the unseen... the vermin.
You have it and I want it!
So tell me, where is it...
Where is the Moon?

I don't know what you're talking about.

...Really.

I swear... I don't have it.

Then tell me...
Why did that dragon tear a hole in the side of your house?

I...

Yes. We felt it all the way down here.
Piqued our curiosity so we came to the surface to see.

Dragons haven't been seen in ages. That dragon could only be after one thing!
We both know what it is, and I want it!

You there!
Get up there and tear her house apart! Don't stop until you find the Moon!

Sire... what about *him?*
What?
He's going to want it when we find it.

NO!
THIS IS WHY I AM KING!!

The power of the Moon supersedes EVERYTHING!

Forget him! He doesn't get the Moon!

He can have her! He can do whatever he wants with her...

...but the Moon is mine!

Eh?
She's free?!
GET HER!!

So many tunnels!
So dark!
How do I get out of here?

Wait! There! It's home!

They're still following me! I won't be able to get up there before they're on top of me!

Maybe I can slow them down!

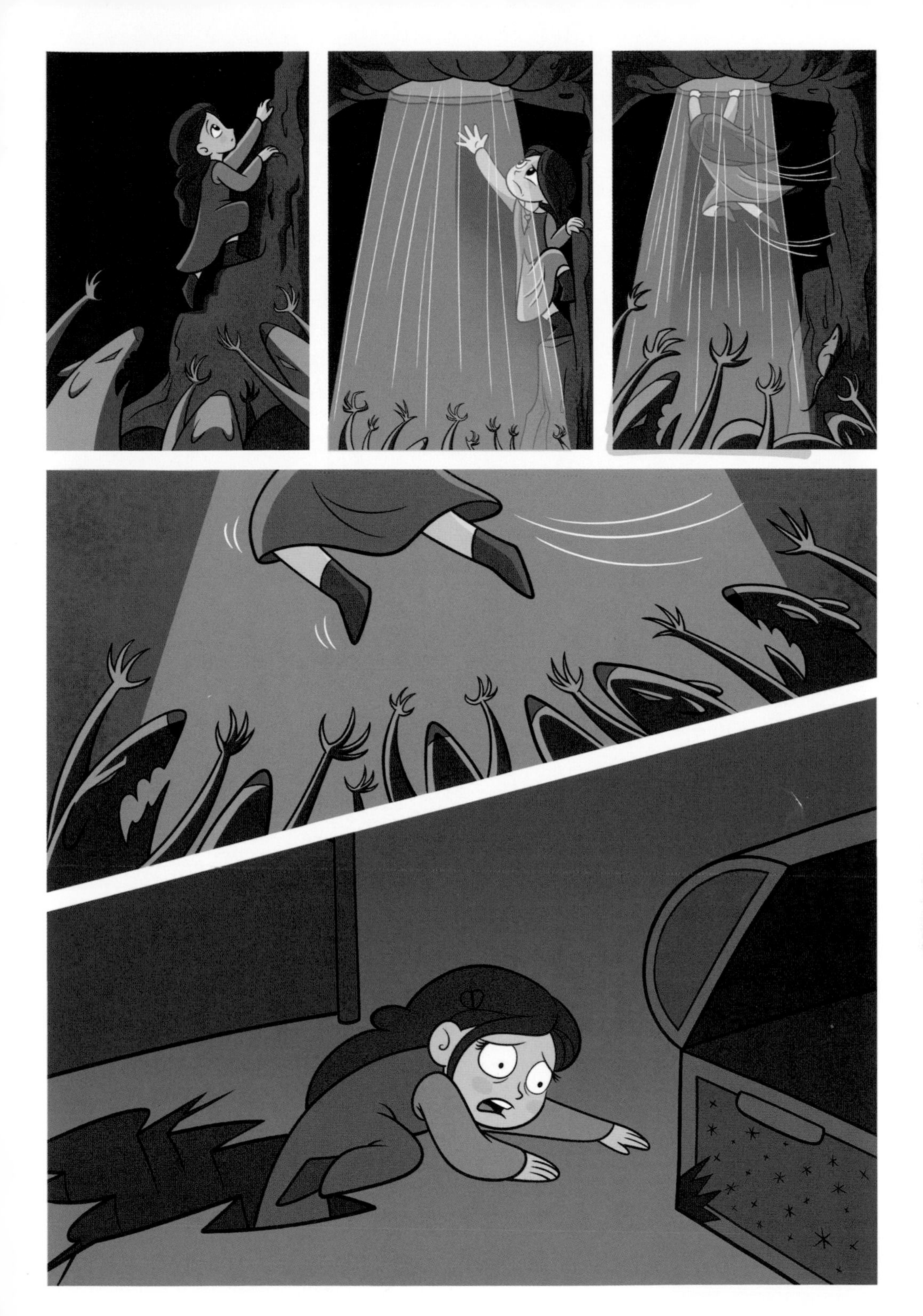

What do I do?
How do I stop them from coming up—

Wait! What's that sound?
Water!
The boiling water I left on the stove!

Please let me be in time! Please!

SPLASH!
Hey! Are you guys here to help us look for the Moon?
Uhhfff!! Come on! Come ON!
Why are we moving?
Uh-oh...

SMASH!

RUMMBBLE!
RUMMBLE!
CRASH!

Soon.
Where is she?
She caved in the tunnel to her house.
We have no access.

BOOGERS you say!
Us... we rats...
...have always been the forgotten creatures!

Throughout history WE have been KICKED AROUND!
HUNTED!
EXTERMINATED!

NO MORE!

THE MOON IS THE POWER WE HAVE BEEN LOOKING FOR!

IT'S TIME WE TAKE IT!
WE HAVE ONE MISSION...

FIND THE MOON!!!

Morning
Sigh.
I don't know why I'm even bothering to clean up...
There's a big hole in the side of the house.
And a huge pile of furniture on the ground I can't lift.
FRIK
FRAK
Not to mention a *rat* infestation.
If it weren't for mom...
I would just leave like everyone else.
But she wouldn't know where to find me if I don't stay here.

I just don't know what to do.

Wait.
What is this?
Where did this come from?

It must have been in the armoire.

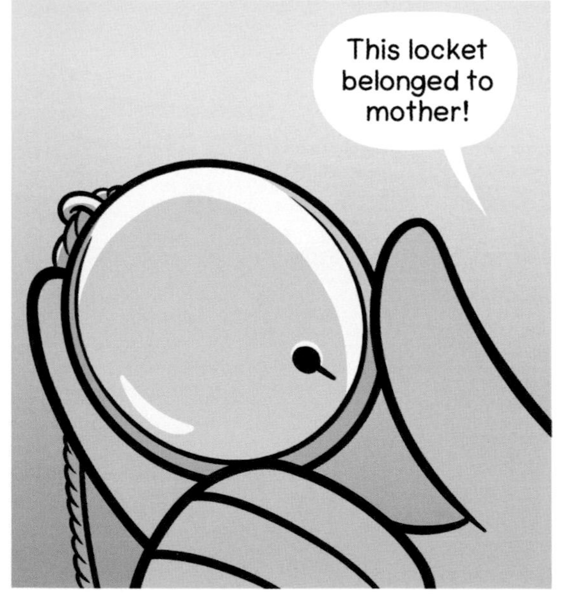
This locket belonged to mother!

The key!
I've looked everywhere for what it might open!
It fits!
A picture of me and...
Sand?
Fae?
Oh!!

Percival!
Fae...
What happened here?
Your house has been destroyed!

It's all a mess, Percival.
And I think I made a *terrible* mistake.

Whatever it is can't be—
You?
It was me.
I took the Moon out of the sky.

What?
I thought Mother...
Wherever she is, would see that it was missing in the sky and come home.

But then the dragon appeared and the rats and—

DRAGON?

It made that hole in the house!

Where's the Moon?
Did the dragon take it?

No. But I don't have it either.
I have no idea where it is.

All of this does answer one question, though.
My mother didn't just leave.
Seeing that creature... I *know* she was taken!

I'm convinced of it more than ever now.

Fae...
Dragons, rats... the missing Moon.
Is it even safe to stay here?

I can't leave.
I won't.

The Moon is nearby. It has to be.
And maybe... maybe my mother is too.

RUUUMMMMMBBLLE!

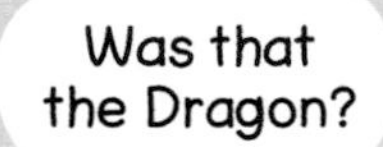
Was that the Dragon?
Did it return?

No...

Then what was that?

I don't know, but my guess is it has something to do with the Moon.

With no Moon in the sky, things will get bad here on the ground.
Earthquakes.
Rising oceans.
Tidal waves.
As time goes by, things will get worse.
I could ask around, see if anyone might know where the Moon might be.
But for your safety, I really feel like you should come with me.
No.
I already told you.
I'm staying.

I need to stay... to make things right.
And for Mom.

I understand.

I'll be back.
Maybe.

I know this little house isn't much, but we can make it a home.
This is our home, but for how long?
Momma?

This belonged to Mother. I think I remember seeing it. She used to wear it around her neck when I was younger.

The armoire...
I should check the crack where I found it.

There's a false back panel.
So that's where the locket was hidden.
Mom's handwriting. This must be hers.
Little Fae and I picked these today
Lucky clover
Fae drawing (age 4)

Plunkett's
Rodent Control
· garlic cloves mashed into a mash
· lavender
· basil
· cut up citrus rinds
· balsam oil and leaves
· soap shavings
· vinegar
· crushed olive pits
· peppermint
Dragon Cake
1 cup flour
1/2 tsp baking soda
1/8 cup vegetable oil
1/4 cup natural peanut butter
1/2 cup apple sauce
1/2 cup pumpkin puree
1 egg
Expand ingreents according to size of dragon.

This one could be useful.
Plunkett's rodent control.
And I have these ingredients... The others I can get from the moon garden.

There's so much in here—
Oh.

The blue rose.
Mom must have put this in here.

It's a good thing I started tending to the garden again.
Wow. These are starting to really perk up.
They look healthy.
I need to work fast. It will be nightfall soon.
There...

That should do it!
Not one rodent will get in this house.

What the—?
How did you two get in here?

Oh no you don't.
You're not welcome here anymore.

Out you go!

And don't even think about—
Uhm...
You remember us, girl?

Mind if I come in?
Ah!
TRIP!
FWOOSH!
What was that?
What are you a magician all of a sudden?

To me, my minions!

You're making this more difficult than it has to be!

BAM!
Give me the Moon!

My King! We can't enter.
There's some sort of protection spell surrounding the entire house!

Impossible!
We're rats! Creatures of the night! There is nowhere we cannot enter!

She can't do this!
It's not going to be that easy!

Because we're not just rats! We're the **Rat HORDE!**

There's got to be more than one way in...
...and the horde can do more than one thing at a time.

You can't stay in there forever!
Uh... sire?

What is it—
Oh boogers!

ROAAARRR!
WUMP!

ROAR!

Where do you think you're going?
Get that Dragon!

ARGGHH!

The sand in
the locket...

It must be
Moon dust!

What did
you do to my
mother?

Where
is she?

Tell me!

Wha—?

Get off
of me!

Oh no!
The locket!

Where
did it go?

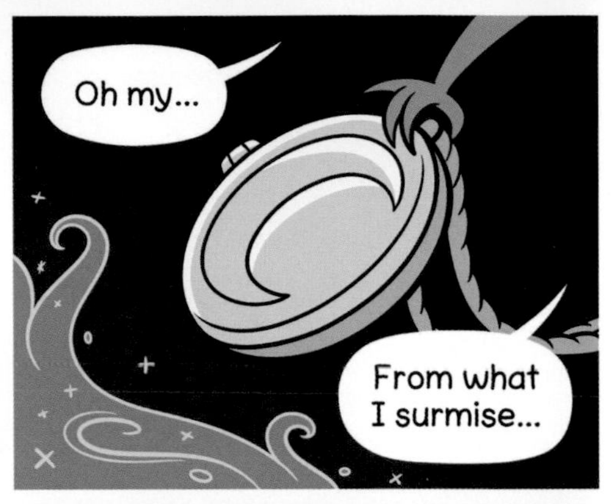
Oh my...
From what
I surmise...

You won't be able
to perform any more
tricks without your
little trinket.

GET HER!

Stop at nothing!
Find that Moon!
Sire...

I don't mean to question your leadership...
...but *he* will want the Moon.

Our biggest problem right now is finding the Moon.

That belongs to us!
I never said I was going to give it to him anyway...

Here!
Give him this!

Maybe that will keep him off our backs for a while.
Once we find the Moon, we will have the power to deal with him permanently.

We have her, sire.
Good! Let's take her down below, so we're not interrupted by anything else. We'll get the truth out of you yet!

Sire!
There's a problem!

What is this?

The tunnels appear to be flooded!
It's filled with black goop.

Fae?

What's happening here?

PERCIVAL, RUN!
Ugh.
These interruptions are becoming tiresome.

I told you I would take care of it.
You haven't.
Not by the looks of it.

Wait...
Percival...?
You're working with the rats?
You're... "him"?
We have news for you, rabbit! You don't get to tell us what to do anymore!
Once we find the Moon, you're—
RUMMMBBBLLE!

RUMMMMBBLE!

What?!
How did you do that?
There's lots of things you don't know about me.
I told you before, Rat—do not cross me.

Percival?
I don't understand.

Poor, poor, Fae.
Of course you don't.

I knew—
Hold on.
RUMMMMMBBBBLE

This belongs to your mother.
I wasn't sure before when I saw that blast of light.

But when these little vermin brought this to me and I looked inside...

I knew what it was.

This is what gives me the ability to make quakes. I've traveled the world and learned much. And one thing I learned was that the Moon would give me powers.

Which brings me directly back to you, Fae.
I want more of what's in this locket... much more.

I want the Moon.
Where is it, Fae?

I don't know. I swear I don't have it.
I don't understand what's going on...

Fae...
Don't take it personally.
I simply want to rule the world.
And the Moon will give me the power to do it.

In the beginning of time there was light.
Giving life to the land.
But when darkness fell each night, that is when the creatures that wanted to rule the planet came out.
They fought and quarreled to lay claim to territories.
Until one day, the "stone" orb appeared in the night sky, no one knowing where it came from. Was it forged? Was it a gift?

Eventually, I found out your mother was the one who placed it in the sky.
She alone had the power to keep it out of reach of all the creatures and monsters.
Making them cower and defenseless. None could hold onto their power.
They slithered back into the darkness.
But there were some that refused to go willingly.
Like me.
I searched everywhere for your mother, and a few years ago, I learned where she was...
And I also learned about you.

I don't believe any of that.
That... can't be true.

But it is...

Even if it is, then why are you after me?

Because your mother was the only one who could bring the Moon back down here to earth...
Until she had a daughter.

KRAK
CRASH!

Percival?

He was no match for me!

A little rabbit?
After my horde destroyed that dragon...
...a little rabbit couldn't stand a chance against the brains and might of the one and only Rat King!

RUMMBBLE!

You can't destroy what you don't understand.

What *are* you?

Ancient. Like the dragon.
Older than most creatures' memories.
You didn't kill me and you didn't kill the dragon.

Ha!
That's what you think!
We are smart and strong!

Me and my kind will be on this planet until the end of time!
We will prevail over you and rule over ALL creatures!

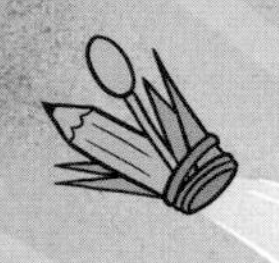
No one can stop me —

STOMP!

I was selfish once, like the rat... was.
But I've since learned to be better.

Look at them scurry away.
That is what fear does.
Oh please...
You're the one who should be afraid, Dragon.
Because of what you did to my mother!
Yes, I may look like a monster, but you are wrong.
The real monster is **that** creature.

You're a silly little girl and I used you.

Your mother fled her old home all those years ago because I was getting close.

She knew there was no way she could protect both the Moon and her new baby daughter.

What if someone were to take the child?

What if they used the child to coerce her to pull the Moon from the sky?

So she told no one of the child. She couldn't take the chance.

It took years to find her.
Another thing I learned from all those years of searching was patience.
I took my time. I planned carefully.
I gained her trust.
Then one night, I put my plan into action. I insisted she pull the Moon from the sky.

You...?
What did you do to her?

She wouldn't give me what I wanted.
I did what I had to do.

No...
NO!

I DON'T BELIEVE YOU!
I KNOW SHE'S ALIVE!
I CAN FEEL IT!
YOU'RE A MONSTER!

Heh.
You want to see what a *real* monster looks like?

Since my first days, I would see the Moon so bright in the sky! All of us night creatures would cower in the depths of our caves away from it's light...

...only to emerge on nights when there was no Moon in the sky. I wondered why it had such much power over us.

Even more so than my species, dragons are susceptible to the effects of moonlight.

But I was smarter than the rest of those inferior creatures.

I made use of my years, learning the mystic arts until I could transform myself and walk into the light.

Don't you see?
I evolved!
I am one of the few creatures, like humans, that can walk in the rays of the sunlight AND in the moonlight.

I used this to my advantage!
Adapting.
Changing.
I've received many monikers because of this...
Forever beast.
Tarasque...
Dragon-Killer.
Hisssss

I was a creature trying to survive.
But I wanted—needed more.
I've seen and done terrible things.
But I've learned how to be most ruthless from humans.
How to deceive, manipulate, steal, and cheat.
I learned all of this by walking among them.

But how could I do this? How could I become ruler over them? I searched for answers, and I learned what sway the Moon held over all creatures.
What I learned most? How much I crave conquering them all!
And I learned just how much power was contained within. The magic it held in its phases. What its light and colors were capable of.
But there was only one problem... I couldn't reach it. Only your mother could wield its power.
So I searched for her.
I found her here with you.
Then it was an easy matter to manipulate you. Use your grief over your mother to get to the Moon.
You can see the power I have with just a bit of Moon dust.
Imagine what I can do with the Moon itself in my grasp! Wield it for whatever purpose I desire! Change its color... Red for Blood Moon carnage! Yellow to sway the power of the seas!

No... she can't be dead.
We have a connection. I would feel it if she were.

It's true. You know it to be true.

I would know if she were gone. She can't be gone.
She would always call me her...

Wait...
Why would you want to change the color of the moon?

ROAR!

You'll pay for what you did to l'Lette!
We'll *never* give you the Moon.
You can try to stop me, Dragon...

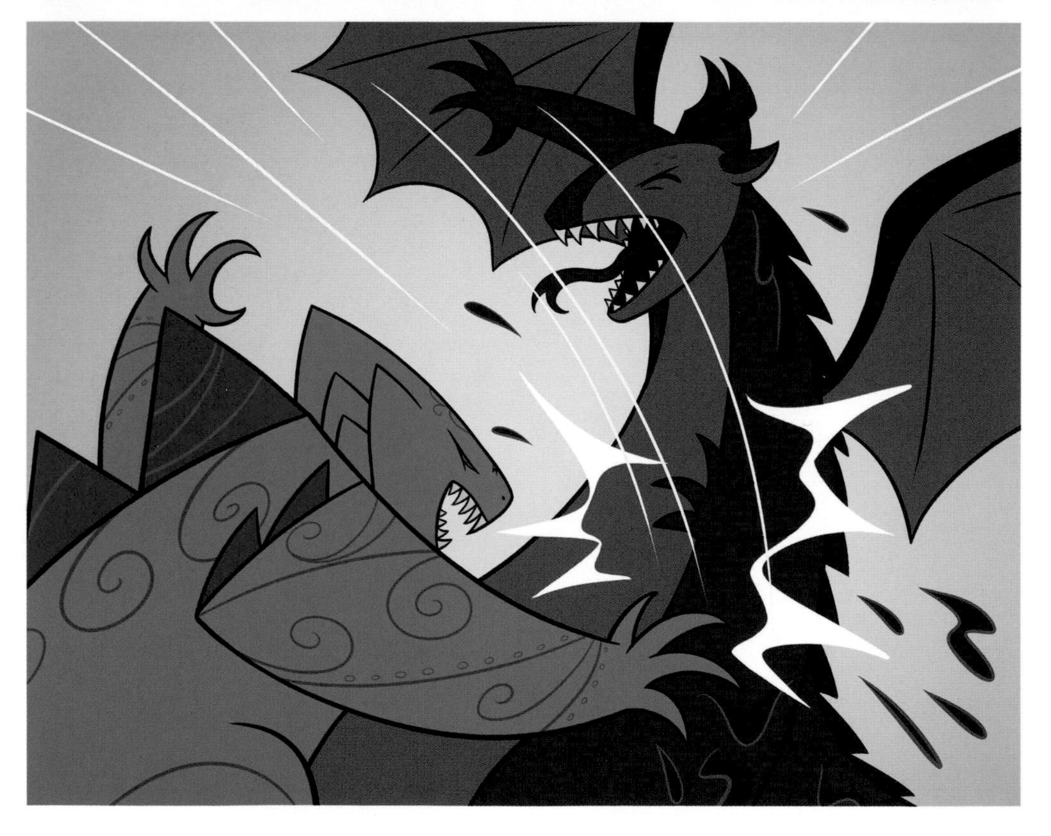

Heh
heh.

The Moon is close! I can feel it!
FLICK

Because your power weakens!
SLAM!

Frik?
Frak?
What?
What are you doing?

The garden? No! We need to get out of here!
Those monsters are destroying everything!

Why are you digging? We can't escape that way.

Wait...
The plants!
They're so big.

How did they get this way?

Oh my!

THE BLUE ROSE!
How?
This is only the second time it's blossomed!

Oh my gosh!

YOU took the Moon!
And you buried it here! In the garden!

What is this?
SLAM!

Pathetic.
All of you are pathetic.
We're not done yet!

ARRRGH!

HUFF
HUFF
Oh no... what have I done?

Done?
You've done exactly as I wanted, child.

SHAKE
SHAKE

Oooof!

I could let you die by the light of the Moon alone, Dragon...
But I think it's only proper that you die at the hands of the "Dragon-killer" as he holds the Moon!

Dragon! I'm so sorry. I thought you were trying to harm me. I thought you took my mother!
RUMMBLE
Is there anything we can do?

There is nothing left that can be done now that he has the Moon.
I'm just so sorry that I couldn't save you... my little sister.

There must be something we—
Did you just call me sister?

I only wanted to protect your mother.
She protected me when others only wanted to destroy me.
She raised me from a hatchling.
Guarded me. Fed me.
Until I could care for myself.
She was a mother to me.
I will always be grateful to her for that.
I'm just sorry I couldn't return the favor and protect you.

I... I didn't know.
I'm so sorry.
How could you know?
She never told you about me to protect you from the likes of him.
Mother held so much power over the Moon.
She would dull its lights on some evenings just so I could fly in the sky with it above me, even though it was difficult for her.
The only thing your mother did was run away to delay the inevitable.
Look at you pathetic fools, meeting for the first time just to have to say goodbye.
But don't worry. Soon you will both be gone, just as she is.

I don't even know your name.
...Kulkan.
The blue flower reminds me of Mother. The stories she would tell of the blue Moon.
I've never seen it... but would have liked to.
People think of flowers as beautiful but frail.
They don't realize the power and strength they have...
Especially this flower.
You are my little blue flower... my Blue Moon!

I hope you're right, mother!

Eh?

What are you doing, Fae?

What are you playing at?

Mom...
I miss you.

HA HA HA!
Your mother can't help you now!

I love you, Mother.

What... what are you doing?

STOP!

This doesn't belong to you!

I see that the blue light of the Moon has no effect on you.
Arrrgh!
But yellow Moon dust still does!
That's my mother's locket!

I'll finish you myself! And as soon as I'm done with you, FAE will be next!

NO!
Mother passed down the power of the moon to me!
I will honor her!

I will make her proud of the person I've become.

ARRRRHHH!

WHAM!
CRACK!
You tricked us!
You lied to us!
You took everything from me!
No, how is this possible?!

THIS IS FOR MY MOTHER!
KRAK!

It's done.
He's done.

Oh, Dragon.
Kulkan...
I'm so sorry.

That "thing" Percival was right.
Mother isn't coming back.
And now I've lost you too.

The horror I've caused by pulling the Moon out of the sky.
I just wanted to feel close to her again.
I wish I could undo all of it.
I know I should put it back.
It's the best way to honor Mother's memory.

But there must be something I can do for you, Kulkan.

There's nothing you can do...

When Mother left... I searched for answers for a long time.

But now I feel I found them. She knew that I was grown and could take care of myself... but you were so young and needed her more...

It was an honor to fight alongside my sister...
Kulkan...?

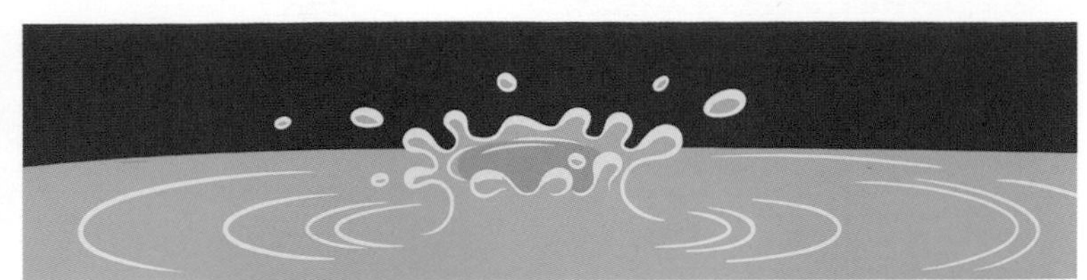

I wish Mother was here.

Fae...
Kulkan?

I-I'm alive! How did you do that?
I didn't do anything.

There was only one blue rose in the garden.
How is this happening?

You.
The power has been in you all along.
How do you think you were able to pull the Moon from the sky?

...Mother?

Oh...
Mother!

You're really here.
How?

You, my dear.
You saved me.

I was fooled by Percival.

I trusted him. He spent years tracking me, gaining my trust.
He wanted me to pull the Moon from the sky for him.
When he realized I was growing suspicious he finally revealed his sinister self. I never could have imagined he was so hateful, frightful inside.

Is that why you dropped the key? Because you were suspicious of him?
You always wear it but I found it in the Moon garden.
Yes. It was just in case... for you. The key to my heart.
When I refused to pull the Moon down for him. He threatened me, he threatened you.
Then he revealed his true visage to me.
He absorbed my essence into himself. Maybe to use my power somehow to get to the moon.
When that didn't work, he turned his attention to you.

Mother. I've been so silly, so foolish. I let him trick me.
I pulled the Moon down.

Don't be ashamed, child.
It's not your fault.
He tricked me for a long time too.

But I'm so proud of how you stood up to him... how you reached for the Moon.

The power does not run through the veins of every generation, but it seems to be within you.

I am happy to see you had some help.
It was the least I could do.

Obviously, the monster could not stand between the combined might of brother and sister.
Now...

This should go back to where it belongs.
I think it's only right that the two of you fly up there and put it back in the sky.

Are you ready, brother?
Most certainly!

All set to go?
I'm so sorry the house was destroyed.

My grief was unbearable when you were gone.

Luckily I had friends that were looking out for me.

Thank you little ones.
I knew I could count on you.

Don't worry about the house. Houses can be rebuilt.
Family is what matters.

And we all have one another.
Where will we go now Mother?
We go find the rest of our family.
Wait...
We have more family?

The Phases of Fae and the Moon

Creating the Characters

Fae

Kulkan

Percival

The Rat King

Becoming a Book

These steps show the development process of a single page from script to sketch to final colors.

1. Script

2. Sketches

3. Final

Finding the Cover

Acknowledgements

Franco Aureliani:

Special thanks to Catherine and Sarah for being my collaborators on this journey. Thanks to Marie Lamba for her guidance in telling me the hows and whys. And to everyone at Little Bee/Yellow Jacket, especially Charlie Ilgunas, for believing in this book, and to all the dreamers and believers out there.

Catherine and Sarah Satrun:

Thank you to Franco for a beautiful story! Thanks also to our friends and family who have been supportive during this whole process. Thanks to Marie Lamba for representing us and making this project possible and to everyone at The Jennifer De Chiara Literary Agency. Thank you to Charlie Ilgunas, Rob Wall, and the team at Little Bee/Yellow Jacket for publishing this project. Also, thank you to our kitties, Charlie and Buster, who kept us company during many long hours in our studio. This project could not have been done without everyone's support!